Bye-bye, Crib

by
Alison McGhee

illustrated by
Ross MacDonald

SCHOLASTIC INC.
New York Toronto London Auckland Sydney
Mexico City New Delhi Hong Kong Buenos Aires

ISBN-13: 978-0-545-14066-9
ISBN-10: 0-545-14066-8

Text copyright © 2008 by Alison McGhee.
Illustrations copyright © 2008 by Ross MacDonald.
All rights reserved. Published by Scholastic Inc., 557 Broadway, New York, NY 10012, by arrangement with Simon & Schuster Books for Young Readers, an imprint of Simon & Schuster Children's Publishing Division. SCHOLASTIC and associated logos are trademarks and/or registered trademarks of Scholastic Inc.

12 11 10 9 8 7 6 5 4 3 2   15 16 17 18/0

Printed in the U.S.A.   40

First Scholastic printing, March 2009

Book design by Einav Aviram

The text for this book is set in Mc Kracken.

The illustrations for this book are rendered in watercolors and pencil crayon, with some letterpress wood type.

To my nieces and nephews: Charlotte Reine
Steiner, William Chiva Blackett, Donald Chivorn
Blackett, McGhee Louise Steiner, Marshall
Washington Steiner, and Evan Caniglia McGhee,
and also to Aunt Judy Schiller

—A. M.

For Quilty and Froggy

—R. M.

This is me.   And this is Baby Kitty.

Pleased to meet you!

I'm a big boy now.
You know what
that means.

No bottle.

No diaper.

And lots of muscles.   Right, Baby Kitty?

Yes, I'm a big boy now.
And big boys sleep in big beds.
Here's what Mom and Dad say:

Bye-bye, crib.

Hello, big bed!

Here's what Baby Kitty and I say:

Not every big boy
wants to sleep in a
big bed.

I'll show you why.
Take a look at that big bed.
That one right over there.

See what I mean?
That's not a big bed.
That's a monster bed.

Do big boys have to
sleep in monster beds?

Even though I might get lost in the sheets
and no one will ever find me again?

Even though my covers might fall off and I'll get frostbite?

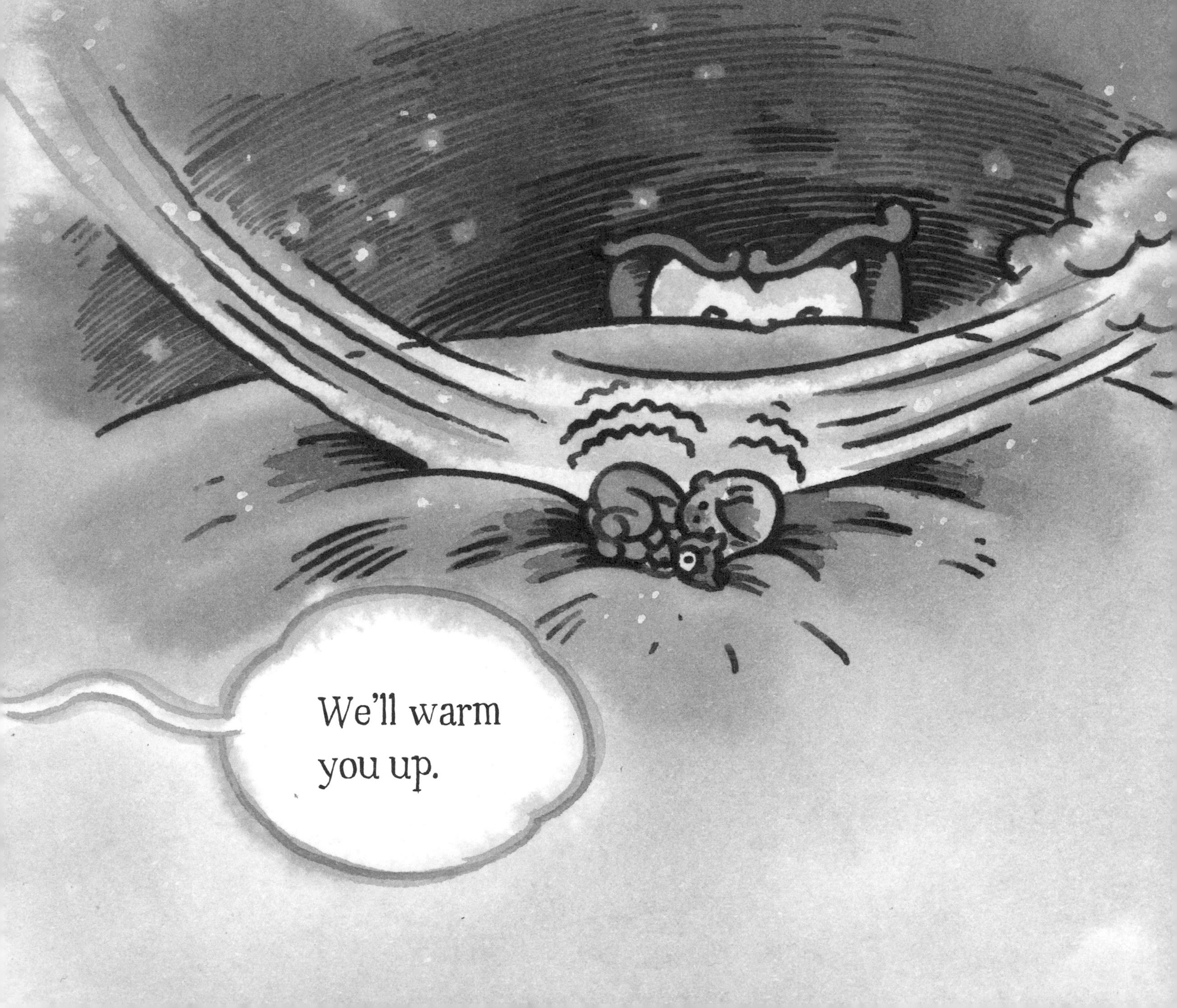

Even if it wants to eat me alive?

Be brave.

What did you say, Baby Kitty?
I can't hear you.
Whisper it in my ear.
You're what?
Oh.

Baby Kitty says he's ready.
Baby Kitty is brave!
If Baby Kitty is ready, then I'm . . .
really ready.

And Red Blankie and Big Pillow look happy over there. Come on, Baby Kitty.
Let's hold paws. You're safe with the muscle boy. Are you ready?

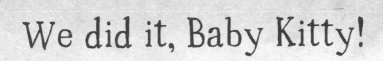

We did it, Baby Kitty!

Let me feel your muscles.
Whoa!
Good-bye,
Baby Kitty.
Hello,
Muscle Cat.

Here's what Baby Kitty and I say:

Muscle cats and
muscle boys sleep in
big beds.

Like this one.

This one right here.